The tale of Lucy Bell who wanted to learn to read and spell

Written by Victoria Devonshire and the Growing Learners Team

Illustrated by Richard Heathcote

ISBN-13: 978-1533445001

ISBN-10: 1533445001

DEDICATION AND ACKNOWLEDGMENTS

For all the children, students, teachers and parents
we have worked with.

We would like to express our gratitude for the Higher Education Innovation Funding,
from the University of Portsmouth, which has enabled us to write this book

Oh I wish I could be like John
He's finished before the bell has gone!
What can I do?
The words just aren't getting through!

Oh I wish I could be like John
I know what reading level he's on!
He knows all his phonemes,
But it's too difficult for me it seems.

Oh I wish I could be like John
A single word he's not forgotten.
He doesn't even have to try,
I would have a go but I am too shy.

Oh I wish I could be like John
If only I could switch my brain on.
The teacher will soon question the class
I hope my seat she will pass.

Oh I wish I could be like John
And just be able to get on.
It's easy for him I can tell,
But I can't read and I can't spell.

Oh I wish I could be like John
My teacher tells me to get on.
But I can't, I will say no
I don't want to have a go.

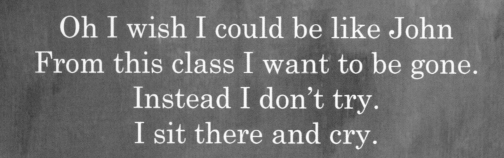

Oh I wish I could be like John
From this class I want to be gone.
Instead I don't try.
I sit there and cry.

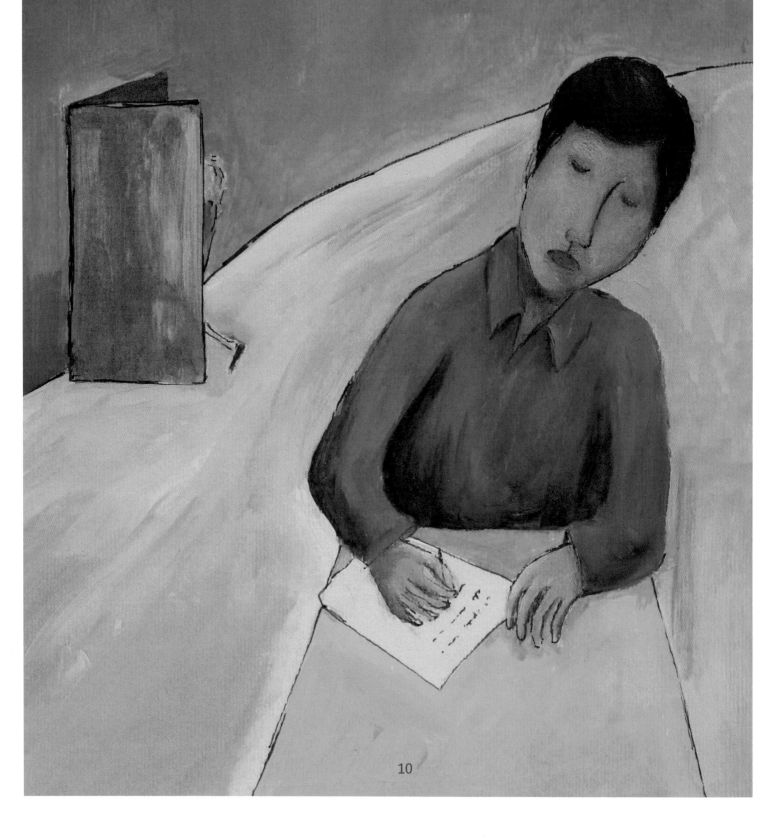

Oh I wish I could be like John
I peek to see what he's working on.
But my teacher did see
And now she wants a word with me.

11

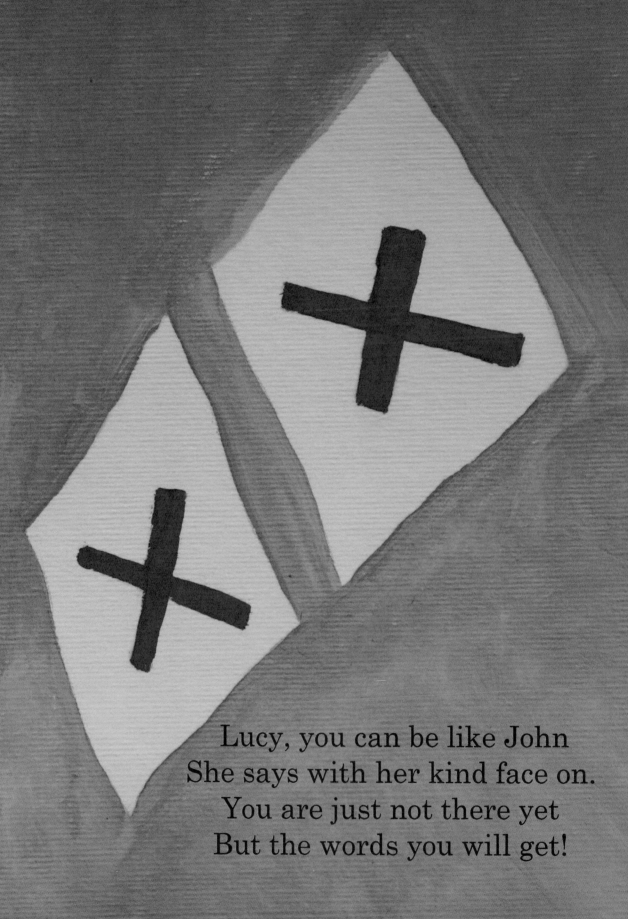

Lucy, you can be like John
She says with her kind face on.
You are just not there yet
But the words you will get!

Lucy, you can be like John
He never gives up, he just carries on.
He tries and does make mistakes
You should see how many he makes.

Lucy, you can be like John
You will soon come along.
Don't worry about making mistakes
It's just practice that it takes.

14

Lucy, you can be like John
He never gives up- just carries on.
He has a growth mindset
That's what you need to get!

Lucy, you can be like John
You will see before long.
All you need to do
Is practice and it will be true.

I can be like John
I'll find new strategies to work on!
I'll give it a go
And I won't say no!

GROWTH

I will be like John
A growth mindset I will don.
I'm not there yet
But to practise I won't forget

MINDSET

I am now just like John
You won't believe the reading level I'm on.
So if you're not there yet,
Remember to have a growth mindset!

QUESTIONS FOR DISCUSSION

What sorts of difficulties did Lucy face at the beginning of the story? Why did Lucy want to be like John?

"It's always easy for John" to read and spell, according to Lucy on page 8. Do you agree with her or do you think that John also struggles sometimes?

Why didn't she want to try and 'have a go' at the beginning?

How did struggling with her schoolwork make her feel?

Do you think that peeking at John's work was a good solution for Lucy?

What advice did her teacher give her?

Do you think John ever makes mistakes?

What did Lucy do after her teacher spoke to her?

What advice would you give to Lucy ?

QUESTIONS FOR DISCUSSION

Do you think that John would have liked to help Lucy? If so, try to imagine a story where John and Lucy have a conversation during lunch break at school.

Do you think Lucy will give up next time she finds something difficult?

What about you? Do you sometimes struggle with reading or spelling? If so, what are your own strategies to do better?

MINDSET LEARNING POINTS

Lucy was having difficulty learning to read and spell and at first she did not want to try.

Lucy looked at another pupil, John, and wanted to be like him because she thought he was just lucky and magically able to read and spell.

Lucy didn't realise that John had worked hard to learn his words. She thought if she didn't know how to do something straight away she would never be able to do it; she thought John was clever and that she was not.

Struggling in class made Lucy feel very sad and she did not want to be there.

She was frightened of making mistakes because she thought that meant she wasn't clever enough and she would never be able to achieve.

MINDSET LEARNING POINTS

When Lucy's teacher told her that it was okay to make mistakes and that even John made mistakes, she realised that she could get better at learning.

Her teacher told her the key to success was practicing, trying different strategies and learning from mistakes; these are the ingredients of a growth mindset.

Lucy adopted a growth mindset and found that with the right effort and strategies she could learn.

Lucy was happy by the end of the story because she knew what to do when she found things difficult. She loves having a growth mindset now!

ABOUT THE AUTHORS

Growing Learners are a team of educational research psychologists based at the University of Portsmouth. We are passionate about supporting schools and parents to improve their children's expectations and attainment, using evidence-based practice to support them to become resilient, confident and effective learners. Everything we offer is underpinned by psychology and education theory, and applied research showing what works.

In designing materials for our intervention packages, we quickly realised that there was a need for children's story books which emphasise the Growth Mindset approach. Dr Victoria Devonshire is a psychologist and member of the Growing Learners Team. She used her experience as a former school teacher and Growth Mindsets researcher, to create The tale of Lucy Bell.

Richard Heathcote, the illustrator, is also a teacher who was very happy to be involved with this Growth Mindset project.

Find out more at: http://www.port.ac.uk/department-ofpsychology/ community-collaboration/growing-learners/

Printed in Great Britain
by Amazon